HORROR WRITERS
ASSOCIATION PRESENTS

POETRY SHOWCASE

VOLUME VIII

HORROR WRITERS
ASSOCIATION PRESENTS

POETRY SHOWCASE
VOLUME VIII

Edited by Stephanie M. Wytovich

Horror Writers Association
2021

HORROR WRITERS ASSOCIATION PRESENTS POETRY SHOWCASE VOLUME VIII

Edited by Stephanie M. Wytovich
http://stephaniewytovich.blogspot.com

Cover by Robert Payne Cabeen
www.omniumgatherumedia.com/robert-payne-cabeen

Interior layout by Eric J. Guignard
www.ericjguignard.com

First edition published 2021

ISBN-13: 978-1-7328035-7-2 (paperback)
ISBN-13: 978-1-7328035-8-9 (e-book)

For information please contact Horror Writers Association
PO Box 56687, Sherman Oaks, CA, 91413, USA
or at: hwa@horror.org

For information on the Horror Writers Association please visit:
www.horror.org

(V101121)

HWA Poetry Showcase Volumes I through
VII are available from Amazon and Kobo

TABLE OF CONTENTS

INTRODUCTION

BY STEPHANIE M. WYTOVICH

THIS IS MY FOURTH AND FINAL YEAR EDITING the HWA Poetry Showcase. As someone who has been involved in this journey from the beginning as a contributor, a judge, and now as an editor, I can't tell you all what an honor it has been to sit beside you, to champion you, and to read and enjoy the nightmares you've submitted. I feel like I've learned so much about poetry, about the horror genre, and most importantly, about our community, and I'm looking forward to taking that knowledge and paying it forward in as many ways as I can, whether that's creatively or perhaps through more of a critical lens.

As I was sitting in my office on campus—a weird feeling after being remote for so long—I was reading this volume again and thinking about the themes that presented themselves throughout this anthology. There is a focus on death, on what's buried, and what refuses to remain hidden. There are also vampires, witches, ghastly creatures, and haunted places (and people). Simply said, in a time when everything is so uncertain, when our health and wellbeing are under siege, the poems within this book became something more than art. They became catharsis, understanding, a funnel for writers to share their anxieties and concerns, their rage and their sadness. There is a stillness within that meets the violence and the dread, and as I read these poems, I was constantly reminded of how horror is a vehicle that allows us to not only contemplate our existence in this world, but process our relationship to the earth, to ourselves, and to our communities.

I hope this book reaches you, that you're able to spend some time *in* these poems and with the lines and images the poets have created. The connection here, the community, is palpable and there's a lot of beauty in that, even if it is clawing its way out ground, teeth bared, stomach growling, hungry for our attention.

For me, this book feels like a little piece of protection magic, a bloodletting, a spell whispered at midnight. It's a good reminder that even when the world looks bleak, when it seems like all beauty and kindness has been lost, that something beautiful can rise from the ashes.

—Stephanie M. Wytovich, Editor

NOTES FROM THE JUDGES

ANGELA YURIKO SMITH

I was honored to serve as a judge for the HWA Poetry Showcase this year—-and what an incredible body of work was sent in! Being a judge for a project like this is like knowing all the good gossip before anyone else does. You see all the brilliant dark poems and poets, but for a little while they are a secret treasure. I've found new favorite poets this year from reading their submissions and then looking them up to read more from them. But now that the collection is published, it's going to be even more exciting to discuss all the new poetry unveiled.

I also love seeing what my fellow judges appreciate in poetry. It's enlightening and therapeutic, as a poet myself, to see what else is being written. Poetry reminds me that we are all in this together, weeping and wondering at similar things, but from different perspectives. This is why poetry is so vital. It builds empathetic bridges between peoples. Through language, we discover that we are different, but share the same burdens.

I find the massive outpouring of creativity sparks my own and inspires me. There's often a synchronicity as current events and trends work their way into the submitted works. The collective poet brain forms a group consciousness that mulls over the events of the recent past mixed with the distant and comes up with a new concoction, a dangerous brew that converts toxicity to tonic. That's the power of dark poetry. When we face fear, when we pin it to the page and bleed the ink from it . . . we walk away empowered.

SARA TANTLINGER

Poetry has been with me for so long. From writing angsty verses in middle school to discovering the world of Edgar Allan Poe to publishing my first collection—poetry has been a constant companion. My poetry publications were actually what allowed me to become an Active HWA member, which is something I continue to deeply value. Being a part of the horror community comes with endless inspiration; I look around and see the triumphs and successes of friends and peers as they pave the road to horror with strong and diverse voices. I am eager to continue to see poetry as an important structure in that road, and the HWA Poetry Showcase is certainly such a wonderful way to do that.

Having the opportunity to read the submitted and selected work was a real joy. The range of ideas displayed on these pages is just a small sampling of what horror poetry has to offer. From nods to iconic characters, beautiful descriptions of the grotesque, unique takes on familiar monsters, and much more, any reader is bound to find something they love within this eclectic group. I am confident readers will enjoy the works as much as we did, and maybe they'll inspire someone who has never written poetry before to give it a try. Congratulations to the selected pieces, and bonus congratulations to the top three featured poems!

Thank you for supporting horror poetry—I know that's something that is incredibly important to everyone who worked on this showcase. Happy reading!

POEMS

CHERRY BLOSSOMS (ON MOURNING A DISTANT MOTHER)

BY E.F. SCHRAEDER

I sit so long on this bench we made of silence
that I forget how to move. Waiting for spring,

the hobbling arrival of this suddenly old stranger startles,
but her cold-air companionship echoes with distant harmonies

and lost relations long strained and soured. Still,
I take the familiar hand, squeeze once for yes, twice no

and listen to the patterned discord of our isolation so like rain,
gliding into an easy banter of half-remembered histories.

No one of us says, this is the last time you see me alive
while spring unfolds in her lush soft petals.

And then I become a wordless shadow of shadows,
a modern-day reaper texting death's final arrival—

seeking companionship, finding no signals, all networks
out of range. No one else grieves what's always been gone.

Each year more desolate, an inching lonely mile, I count
twenty reasons we walked that narrow path. Each, a mistake.

RESTLESS SPIRITUALISTS

BY AMANDA HARD

We are teaching the dead to speak
our language, *once for yes; twice
for no*. Providing instructions:
the table to rap, a candle to flicker.

The parlor, draped in black, mirrors
and windows covered, we are transforming
into a playroom with trumpets, a drum,
paper and crayons, a wooden spirit board.

We are teaching the dead to hear
beneath our questions, the hesitation;
forever training them not to respond
to what we ask, but what we need.

Although the dead have little interest
in toys, in conversation, still we try
trick upon trick to convince ourselves
we have been given all that we implore.

We are hoping the dead will feel
pity for us, will answer when we call

out in the blackest night, our dark hour,
to ask for light. And yet—

The flame remains still, the table silent.
Our dead have nothing left to say.

RUN AWAY

BY ROBERT PAYNE CABEEN

Be vigilant, the night is still and warm.
The arthropods are hatching, run away.
The restless city sleeps as mutants swarm.
Beware—insect behavior—run away.

In search of food, ants big as cars,
With pincers stout and keen,
Explore the urban underworld,
In service to their queen.

The reeking blood chum carnage on the street
Attracts them by the hundreds, run away.
Ants roam by night in search of something sweet.
They'll surely sniff your sugar, run away.

From where they came, I cannot say,
But one thing is for sure,
Their hunger is insatiable,
And none of us secure.

It's hard to keep from screaming when you hear
Their pinchers slash and flay defenseless prey.
Those mutants have a frightening ear for fear.
They're quick and cunning—run, run, run away.

SHADECREST PALISADES

BY MANNY BLACKSHER

Twelve fired trash barrels char the green night
Eleven dust halos gild sodium lights
Ten stoned-out windows that blind the old gym
Nine gates grace the church that remembers no hymn
Eight iron players who stake the estate
Seven scarce welchers whose payments are late
Six red-eyed patrolmen who prowl on the take
Five evening ladies who lie in the lake
Four funeral parlors with Singapore lace
Three nameless vagrants who cover their face
Two hungry babies who scream until morn
Sounding the shadows, the Man with the Horn.

ALL OF THE GHOSTS ARE GONE

BY CHAD HELDER

And then all of the ghosts were gone,
the population hunted down much like
sperm whales and buffalo,
paranormal investigators coming up empty,
EVPs even more silent than the grave
is purported to be.

As greedy as anteaters, the ghost junkies
snorted and sucked all the ghosts away,
swallowing the wandering spirits,
huffing even the most kinetic poltergeists.

They emptied out the best ghost hunting locations:
the elementary school library
where a bomb once exploded,
the charred children playing
spectral duck duck goose no more;
the abandoned mental hospital where
pioneering practitioners of brain slicing
silenced many voices,
even the phantom voices silent now.

So many ghosts out there, how could we run out?
You would be shocked how fast it went.
Remember the buffalo.

Ghost junkies claim:
such a spiritual rush to suck up a specter.
So great, most paranormal investigators
have turned.

Soon the ghost junkies will need more ghosts,
all of the haunted houses just houses;
soon the only ghosts available to eat
will be those walking around
inside blood and meat.

LUCKY CHARM

BY CYNTHIA PELAYO

Voices seep in through cracks in the drywall, and
This is how it works, the reverberations of terror
Shaking, quickened breaths blessed by rolling tears
I smile, close my eyes and am filled with your screams
Cry louder, I plead silently. For some time, I listen
To faint breaths, followed by your whimpers, tapping
And tinkering with loose threads of rope unraveling
Between fingernails, but in darkness hopelessness
Saturates, consumed within cramped spaces, moaning
Echoes along corridors behind wood and electrical wire
Repeated back to you, and so, I wait, and I relish the
Silent sounds of first refusals and then defeat, a pulse
Quickens before it ceases, a body beneath floorboards
Or standing erect behind one's basement wall, like Poe's
Tell-Tale Heart or his Cask of Amontillado, energizes
A house, reinvigorates an eternal scream bottled and
Sealed, you and your death are my good luck charm
Like a desiccated cat lined within the walls of a new
Home to ward away evil spirits, or perhaps it's even
Like a dried chicken's foot tucked within the attic
Intended to bless and protect from negative energies
But I prefer my homemade spell, you my exquisite
Mummified corpse radiating energy in my walls that
I will convert and store, my lovely Witch Bottle, wrapped
In roses and ribbons, cloves and rosemary, and lemon
Grass. One last struggle, and your movements stop
Your screams will eternally empower me and this house

REVELATION 9:15

BY BENICIO ISANDRO

On a withered farm forlorn,
the lonely stable stood—
an ancient one from yore
with floors of rotting wood.

The lonely stable stood
fast with weathered walls.
Its floors of rotting wood
bore sigils quickly scrawled.

Fast in weathered walls,
the little one slumbered
with sigils quickly scrawled
on corpses torn asunder.

The little one slumbered
in swaddling made of flesh,
from corpses torn asunder,
inside a grisly nest.

In swaddling made of flesh,
the sleeping infant grew.
Inside that grisly nest,
its wings were made anew.

The sleeping infant grew
into the Angel sent to kill.
Its wings were made anew;
its piercing cry was shrill.

The Angel, sent to kill,
descended on us all.
Its piercing cry was shrill:
the herald of our fall.

Descending on us all,
the ancient One from yore
heralded our fall
from a withered farm forlorn.

THE TO-DO LIST THAT NEVER ENDS

BY KERRI-LEIGH GRADY

Get the kids fed.

Encourage them to hurry. It's getting late.

Run to the mall for a new aquarium nightlight so the kid will sleep.

Get the kids to the car. It's dark now, and they still need a bath.

Figure out what you want for dinner tonight. Wine? Probably.

> Answer the question from the man behind you: "Late night shopping?"
>
> Turn so you can watch the strange man while you get the kids in the car.

Need to do some laundry before dinner.

Strap in the baby while he arches against the buckle.

Pull the nightlight out of the stroller so it will fold.

> Respond to the man when he says: "Well, see you later."
>
> Note the crawl of foreboding across your scalp and your gut screaming to run.
>
> Watch him drive away, the wrong direction on a row with slanted parking.
>
> Look around the empty lot for help.

Tell the older kid to climb over his brother and get in his seat.

Ask the older kid to buckle himself.

Take a deep breath when he says he can't.

Close the van door.

13

Try to fold the stroller that never goddamn folds the first time.

Don't curse—the kids will hear your fear.

Consider the price of a new stroller if you leave it, back over it on the way out.

Consider the bank account.

Sigh with relief when it collapses.

Throw the damned thing in the back.

Slam the back door shut.

> See the man has driven around to the next row.
>
> See that he's parked directly in front of your car now.
>
> See through the sparse shrubs that his brights are on, spotlighting you, obscuring him.

Calculate the distance to the driver's door.

VISITING HOURS

BY VINCE A. LIAGUNO

Alone
in an ever-shrinking box
with a porthole that teases
a freedom from droplet precautions
and the smell of disinfectant.
Isolated
amongst other elder tribesmen
who, too, have traveled long roads—
taken paths less chosen—
and now converge at this crossroads.
Sequestered
within pandemic pandemonium
where snippets of worry filter through the air
like the microscopic contagions
that seek entry through masked cavities.
Alienated—
cut off and set apart—
compartmentalized by sickness and syndrome,
in a suffocating casket
where space and time seem endless.
Disaffected
by social isolation
when the sliding glass doors
closed for the last and final time
and even that couldn't keep the monsters at bay.

Quarantined
as the virus stalks darkened corridors
that no longer ring out with shouts
of "Bingo!" or birthday song refrain
and even the ring of call bells has gone silent.
Reconciled
as the (wo)man in the puffy astronaut suit
announces that I finally have a visitor,
and I instinctively open my mouth in acquiescence
to at last receive my host.

BURIED

by Lindy Ryan

Broken bodies
pressed under wet earth,
cocooned in rags
stained red as life drains
into the hungry dark—

Food for maggots
that suckle at eyeballs,
weave through graying flesh
and brittle bone,
fed by the hungry dark—

Dirt under nails
still soft, still crumbling,
dim against pale flesh,
a memory of you
lost to the hungry dark—

THE SERPENTS' TALE

BY LISA MORTON

Beneath the City of Angels
(a place of heated shadows)
they sleep, in rooms of golden walls,
in halls paneled with stories
of the glories
before the warmblooded came,
with skin in place of scales,
nails where they have claws.
They dream of that future
when they rise,
when their slitted eyes
once more expand and hypnotize.
Their shimmering tails will wrap,
their venomous fangs sap life.
Amid the strife,
the City of Angels will drown
in hot red blood and cold emerald moultings,
and the serpents will once again rule
from trees of knowledge.

THE SONG OF THE WANDERING ZOMBIE

BY GRAHAM MASTERTON

If I should rise again
If I should rise
To walk the paths where once I walked alive
And see the sun again and feel the wind
And where the summer starlings wheel and dive

I'll have no greed for sinew or for bone
I'll have no hunger for another's flesh
My life is past
My days are gone
They have their life ahead of them to live afresh

But—
Slow and unsteady I will climb their stairs
Dragging the sheets I've carried from my grave
Even if they awake I will be masked
My grey skin, and my grimace, and my eyes like caves

And I will lie
And I will lie so close to them.
I'll cup their exhaled breathing in my hand
So I can share the day they've had—the kisses
And the laughter and the wine
The breaths that I once took, when I was living in the land

THE SILENCE OF GOD

BY JAMAL HODGE

Words.
The original dream.
Upon his tongue,
...*tasted*...
unseen.

Wet words.
Forced through,
bacteria caked spaces.
...*Behold*...
His bloody teeth.

Aged words.
Death his lips.
Pass,
kissed,
...*drifting*...
unseen.

Lost words.
Without from within.
Not his children,
Nor his kin.
Are we,
...*the answer*...
...*or the scream*...
The tears,
in God's

dream?

TEETH

BY BRAD CHRISTY

Click, pop, click along the bicuspids
Floss slips and slices around the incisors
Sawing back and forth until the string is stained red
Without teeth, animals wither in the wilderness
Destined for disease, death and decay
Or the ravages of being ripped apart
By something that still has its teeth
I spit red sputum into the sink
My cracked lips stretch over my gums into a grin
Click, pop, click, I lick crimson from my canines
I imagine prey walking down paved paths
Tender morsels talking on telephones
Their savory scents send shivers across my skin
Biting nourishes this body
Hunger having replaced humanity.

THE MADNESS OF MONSTERS

BY SHELDON WOODBURY

There are dreams within dreams and mysteries within mysteries
but the tattered bond that connects them all are the nightmares
that weave an infinite tapestry of horror and fear

Molten ash swirled around its twisted horns and gargantuan wings
as it strode a withered necropolis of blistering misery
a raging behemoth ruling the underworld

Then its wretched wasteland of torture and pain was suddenly gone
leaving it all alone in a shuddering void of howling darkness
the shudder was fear then it was gone too

Which brings us to another realm but this one is different
glittering and radiant high above ruled by a supreme being
with the arrogant belief it had created it all

Angels swooped and soared in the wispy white clouds
as a mysterious whisper crept into its godly mind
revealing it was a monster too made out of madness

Then a brutal and shocking atrocity occurred
angels were ripped from the clouds in splattered pieces
the rest of its heavenly realm was obliterated too

But all this was just the musings of another monster
lurking in one of the unknown universes that stretched forever
its shivering eyes like celestial black holes

A whisper slithered in just like before
to comprehend the terror it felt is only possible
if you've glimpsed the nightmare beyond cosmic insanity

Size is power and insane power is the ultimate fear
it had always thought it was the biggest and scariest monster ever
but now it knew it couldn't have been more wrong

VARGAS VISITS THE MONASTERY (A VAMPYRE SPEECH)

BY PATRICIA GOMES

"Let there be light," He commanded,
and the universe opened to spread
intrusive tendrils of shimmering gases.

We were frightened.

Before light, there was only
obscurity.

And being obscure,
we thrived.

We are
before time;
your millennia are our days. Your eons,
our seasons.
Gods of the stars,
we walk in reverse, unseen.

Our teeth were honed in deserts
on the thick-furred necks of megafauna.
Our bodies oiled
by bejeweled, brown-skinned women
who fed us perfumed children.

There, before time,
I saw the dawn of your beliefs,
witnessed the first placement of the Palm,
eavesdropped on and spurned the robed men
who plotted new Scripture,
carving their symbols into animal hide,
but never
have I seen the eyes of Christ.
No—
I've never seen Him at all.

OUR NIGHTLY VOYAGE

BY AMY LANGEVIN

The night calls me to her palace.
Its walls are shining steel and filled with frosty air.
She waits on a bed strewn with dead amaryllis.

Candles illumine her, my dear, sweet Alice.
I kiss her frozen lips, stroke her dark, silky hair.
The night calls me to her palace.

Lovingly, she listens, her eyes gray as stratus.
Her arms cradle me with boundless care.
She waits on a bed strewn with dead amaryllis.

We grow warm, our eager limbs entwined like lattice.
I lie her back and spread thighs so smooth and fair.
The night calls me to her palace.

I sink into her, parting slippery callus.
Death grips life. Heaven flares.
She waits on a bed strewn with dead amaryllis.

Heaven explodes, filling me and my sweet Alice.
Our souls rise, clasp hands, and flee the human nightmare.
The night calls me to her palace.
She waits on a bed strewn with dead amaryllis.

AFTERLIFE

BY MERCEDES M. YARDLEY

When you fall in love, they say,
it's for better or for worse
until death do you part

But what about when death comes
With its teeth bared
To grab you by the throat and
shake

You're left holding a crumpled hand in the dark

How do I cease loving you simply because your lungs
don't draw air the same way
or to be honest, really at all

Your big, beautiful heart still turns my world
even when you are
-quite literally-
wearing it on your sleeve
with the rest of your viscera

One virus to your system or bullet in your skull
doesn't make you less deserving of my love
So, my love

I'll hold you through your death throes
I'll hold you as your blood flows
and as your body struggles to stand

I'll take your corpse by the hand and we'll
Walk into the night together.

IN A PLACE SOMEWHERE INSIDE

BY RONALD J. MURRAY

Where agony strides to self-devour,
She hides in a fold and crease
Of darkness kept in depthless corners,
Where wept an angel in dreamless sleep.

And she taunted me like moths amused
At my haunted, partial cocoon,
From where I watched convulsing love
Gasp to drown itself in hemlock tea.

I captured the sounds in decanters
To drink myself to stagnant deep.
Like panicked songs of strangled doves,
I shrieked like a dog to the breeze.

YOUR EYES, UMBER DARK, A DISEASE

by Lonnie Nadler

Your eyes, umber dark, a disease
Mine, midnight pale, infected with your look.
Your touch, a torrid poison
Running through me, never enough.
Your name, an incantation
Casting memories of years yet come.
Your black satin hair, at war
With my cotton neck, forever marred.
Your lips are stillness, stiff corpses
That mine long to tend—and dissect.

TO NECROPHILIA

BY Katherine Kerestman

Oh rosy Dawn, ye bright blush of heaven's
Angels who behold my loveliest paradise—
Celestial spirits are envious even
Of my Necrophilia's emerald eyes.

Living maiden, thy glance is sorcery,
Enchants, captivates, ensnares, enslaves
Mortal man in thrall to thy mystery,
Conqueror conquered, lord reduced to knave.

None power hath my cold love's sparkling jewels
In her soft. smooth, still alabaster brow
To influence, dictate, direct, nor fool
Her lord to thrall of bride—deceased now.

Ne'er more shall wield such sweet sorceress glances,
Pallid marble stirs this poet's senses.

SEEDLING

BY BEVERLEY LEE

She sees so clearly in the dark
Uncluttered by the clumsiness of sight.
Strange comfort in this bed of wholesome earth
Amidst the pulpous, miry writhe.
Sweet slithers in her soul
Tethered here in her glass castle
She dreams of black-winged swallows
taught to dine upon the wing,
longs to lap the juice of death,
to stain herself with crimson.
Sweet sip of sacred scarlet
Soon he will come to marvel
Caress her skin-soft petals,
The rippling elegance of leaf.
Seedling he used to murmur
And she thought it charming,
An outpouring of a tender heart
Until she was transformed.
Sweet scrap of Girl remains
A breath of night upon a silken stigma
she bends her slender neck
sends her scent to coil and probe
And waits.
This starving hunter will be fed
Unfettered by the flaw of flesh and bone.

THE UMAMI OF BLOOD

BY MICHAEL ARNZEN

the umami of my blood
seeps into your tongue sponge—
the delicious spice of sin

saturate

lick too, this tumorous turmeric
from the cardamom corpses I've killed,
rub the rancid raw brisket

with its rich platelets, its pink plasma—
a pleasing bedtime dish
simmering for my cannibal carnivore

satiate

lover, drizzle this over your dessert
and if you can
let the red velvet rivulets
cake overnight

your morning manifests
in an unbridled breakfast
slaked by your overbite

reanimate

salivate

taste me

LONG FORGOTTEN

BY EV KNIGHT

In a dark, neglected alley
Felled among the litter of life which continues oblivious to
A vessel long forgotten, abandoned to vices, addiction, and quid-pro-quo "love"
Deeds once done in displeasure, memories that hound at hearts and minds.
Nothing more than a box of chocolates hardened with age
Or a once sweet-smelling perfume soured by abuse and disregard
Leaking from the dented, rusty corner is neither love turned to indifference
nor passion spoiled by neglect
But a rancid, congealing stew of jealousy, vengeance and maybe, one day, regret.
Time is the chef thickening with coagulants—a gelatinized puddle on dirty cement
Cats and rats and insects make a meal of the clot while
The bruised and indurated body within stiffens
Blood once flowing warm and thick now cold and curdled
Long forgotten

WE ARE BORN OF BLADE AND BLOOD

BY NACHING T. KASSA

I trembled as the blade fell,
It carved the air above me,
And severed the slender cord,
Which held me to the earth.

They lifted my head high,
A fist clenched in my hair,
I gaped at the crowd below,
Tasting an iron taint of death.

Half of me in the dirt,
Staring at my cruel madame,
Her thirst for blood unquenched,
Slicing many a pale neck,

Darkness ended torment,
Greasy torchlight flickering,
I shut my eyes and woke,
To a stranger in my grave,

I scream in silence,
Calling to my other half,
Ghostly pain of cobbled streets,
Beneath my once bare feet.

DEATH MASK

BY STEPHANIE ELLIS

I could wait until you fade
and your final farewell
whispers on my cheek

mould an impression
in plaster
cold reminder
pale imitation of life
to hang on my wall

or

I can take the face
of you

alive

slide your flesh
from its scaffold
fold you up
in my pocket

a scalpelled portraiture
to be warmed
by my heat

my memento mori
an organic tissue
to wipe away sin

EPIALES

BY CAITLIN MARCEAU

I like watching
in the dark
when you unzip your flesh
expose your demons
bare your soul
if you had one.

I like thinking of you
late at night
when your bones heave
crack wide open
down to marrow
sucked dry.

I like tasting it
under my nails
when your insides teem
spill onto the floor
soak through Earth
made red.

I like feeling it
on my tongue
when your breath pours out
thunderously quiet
a war drum
struck silent.

NIGHT OUT AT THE OLD CIRCUS

BY IAN HUNTER

It was a mistake to come here
Creeping past the clown sitting on the wooden crate
who looks dead, drunk, asleep
head resting on his chest
a flaccid red thing spread across his leg
which might have been a balloon once

The impalers on stilts are very quick
Despite their height
They balance on long wooden legs
Kill with long wooden stakes
protruding from frayed jacket sleeves

The knife thrower will have an eye out
Before he gets his eye in
The straw is blood-matted
The wheel is blood-spattered
and gouged with the bite of a knife

NIGHT OUT AT THE OLD CIRCUS BY IAN HUNTER

They call the row of young people The Scream Keyboard
stretched across the centre of the ring
Outstretched arms and legs pegged to the ground
No gags for them
their cries and pleading need to be heard
along with the screams and other sounds
they make as the elephant walks across their bodies

You are the last one left
Hearing the swish of the impalers'
pointy arms behind you
the clown's head turns as you run past
before he eases off the crate
a grin on his face, arms outstretched
following you into the night

DEAD AS BRAINS

by Lorna D. Keach

A long high table set with bowls,
each one full, brimming, the dark lit with candles,
and you think you're supposed to be here,
you think: it's tradition.

The bowls: ceramic and porcelain,
slick lacquered, burnished clay,
they hold during other rituals,
mashed potatoes, rice, spaghetti, heaps of warm comfort.

The table: much taller than you,
an adult table, and you think:
I'd made it here already, after years and years
of kids' tables, folded legs, plastic gingham sheets in red
checkerboards. Now this table is long-legged, oak-dark
and cold

(you are feeling cold, up on tippy-toes)

and you remember when someone first told you hell
was actually cold, a frozen lake, and you thought
that was the end of your childhood. Only children
think of hell as a fiery pit, tables as small and collapsing,
potatoes-peas as castles buried

in moats of gravy. Children think in spoons and plates and
    manners and devils
and fiery pits, but adults think in bowls and oak and cold.
    Adults eat with their hands

(the adults are eating now, with their hands)

Behind you, a soft push, as if to say,
be an adult,
as if to say,
remember the lake of ice

Someone whisper-giggles *it's only cold*
spaghetti, and you sink your fingers
down into the bowl and the cold
and you ask *what's inside?* but you know.
You know.

CARRIE

BY EMMA J. GIBBON

Steam and dreams and estrogen,
your hand between freckled thighs.

The white rafts that sailed toward you,
would not save you,
would not stop the bleeding
no matter how they clung to your leg.

Prom-dress-pink was never your color,
always red, even in split screen.

Your problem was your mother.
Isn't it always?

HOW DATE NIGHTS BRING YOU EVER CLOSER (A FORBIDDEN HAIBUN)

BY TERRIE LEIGH RELF

discovering new ways
to bind us together
illuminated manuscripts

How we replay them over and over again: classic horror films. New
neighbors stop by, but never leave . . . take-out order canceled.

developing a taste
for full-bodied wine
metallic overtones

Howling through the night . . . that moon, that glorious blood moon.
Death by a thousand kisses: resurrection.

bathing each other
with white oleander soap
evisceration dance

CAREFULLY TENDED HORRORS AND GARDENS

BY TRISHA J. WOOLDRIDGE

Let me tend my movie monsters,
    garden my gothic ghosts,
      bloom roses of arterial spray.
Let me paint my façade of gore with gorgeous purpose
over this grotesque house of warped mirrors
reflecting the illusion of lost control.
Myself and not myself—not really—
More real.
More real than real-mirror lies
    reflecting my made-up clown mask,
hiding horrors inside my skin,
my mind.
Bonafide blood-and-tissue-smeared thighs,
    authentic, purple-bloomed bruises
      make certified doctors recoil, turn away.
My own ghost fades in once-loving eyes.
Whispers weave security for actual monsters,
    within their hunting ground of HOA-perfect homes—
all full of decoratively shattered mirrors
    reflecting the illusion of control.

A GARDEN OF FLESH

BY DEBORAH L. DAVITT

The flower mouths
that sprouted from my flesh
murmur a constant chorus
disagreement, disharmony;

red like roses
blooming against
the skin of my wrists,
petals always opening,
closing, winking
their stamen eyes
knowingly.

Whispering
just under my ears
where they twine up
from the flesh of my throat,
whispering of all their hungers;

their thorns dig into
the very flesh they grow from,
drawing blood—
it hurts to deny them,
they make sure of that—

From under my skirt
a soft, inviting chorus;
it would be more embarrassing
if I didn't know
just how many thorns
grow down there, too—

such a hungry garden
I have for you.

A WOMAN'S WEAPON

BY KC GRIFANT

In the botanist's garden
A leafy offshoot reaches, like a hand, suppliant
along the wrought iron table where he takes his tea

The botanist trails his calloused thumbs
along the folds of her frond.
Nicolle: a testament to his talents, a flash of ferocious fuchsia among
    the verdant

Every night he talks to her,
Every night he thinks
of her leaves uncurling

She bleeds bitter essences to make him itch;
builds barricades of barbed thorns.
But he'd put on his stained yellow gloves and
trim
her
back.

Nicolle had once been forged of femurs and freckles.
When they met, he envisioned unfurling his muscles into hers.
But she had shot him down, sheared his dreams, so

He infused a concoction of his raging rejection into a bouquet.
Nicolle arranged the anonymous blooms, not seeing how
Their chemicals coerced her cells to morph and contort.

He found her later,
Bones splintering into stalks
Wet eyes whorling into pristine petals.

Now he sits, sipping.
Watching Nicolle's tendrils unwind toward him
like he had always hoped.

The botanist doesn't see
the trail of insect bodies beneath her drooping leaf,
her toxic tainted shimmer turning toward his tea.

GIRLS WHO CREATE MONSTERS

BY JEANNINE HALL GAILEY

Cannot be the shape of
tender   glamour   softness gloss
what could be   what they want somehow
completely out of reach

Instead girls create body parts sewn together
animated   without   love
eroding lofty unstable

collect bones   hair   insects on pins
relics of   a history
a hunt   for evidence

Alone in a landscape
of death plague blood fire senescence
of course girls   so well acquainted

with sickrooms   bleeding with losing
        with bodies that do not cooperate
in the dark with fear   the shadows that devour

our monsters   haunt your hallways   your
    dreams
we are acquainted with the horrors inside us
we nightmare we bleed we burn we decay we are buried
    strangled

you may rewrite our stories
but our monsters will not die
we continue to sing them into being

SUGAR

BY JACQUELINE WEST

Sweetness is what they expect of us.
Little girls, kindly mothers,
dear old ladies in pantries and flowerbeds;
petit fours and gingerbread,
icing on our fingers, honey on our tongues.
They expect the lure of blossoms,
the scent of fresh-baked temptation,
the candy path to the unlocked door.
They expect our gifts. And when they take,
it's without asking, grasping fistfuls,
breaking glass and ripping walls.
We're just too sweet to resist.
Somehow they never see it coming:
the gate that closes, the cage that clasps.
The moment when we demand payment
for all that they've already stolen,
the proof still sticking to their lips.
But honeybees sting. Little girls bite.
Old ladies have kitchen knives.
We have appetites too, and our teeth
are sharper than they are sweet.

RITUAL FOR REUNITING WITH MY FAVORITE DEMON

BY KAILEY TEDESCO

when the cornstalks shucked blood-splatter & the sky curdled,
i felt the ceremony's unfurling—heart-plucked in apocalypse
lipstick, i untwist the tryst-blade from my index finger
to witness your deliverance: as a girl, you wore bibbed-
lace &, envious, i scribbled the contents
of your locket, scribbled your night-prayers un-naughty
in order to become possessed again. once exorcised,
i missed you dearly—the way you burned clocks
backward, let time fungus my dress. separate,
we unzipped at the pelvis & ribs. i tucked the idea
of you into my bedsheets, cut cavities for eyeballs
& longed for your sobs. a split end, all i know
is peeled from me—with a mirror in my mouth,
i pretend we share a tongue, cake-frosted with death.

WIN, LOSE

BY DONNA LYNCH

This is my favorite, awful game
My opponent is the dark
A game of odds
A game of wait and see
A game of chance

Standing late at night
with my back turned to the ocean
where anything could drag me in
and drown me in the shallows

Gazing at the rising mist
along the pitch-black lakeshore
where any nightmare figure could appear
and suddenly give chase toward the door

Looking out of naked windows
into the new-moon woods
where anyone could see me
and I would never know as they approach
Swimming in clears waters
where the sea floor falls away
where the trenches turn the tides
and turn us into prey

WIN, LOSE BY DONNA LYNCH

Peering into endless canyons
the abyss cries out so loudly
in answer to my silent call
the one I don't know why I make

Staring in the mirror
studying my features
because I know I am not me
I know that I am gone

I play my favorite, awful game
and I don't know if I've lost or won
just that the game goes on and on
until someday the moment comes
when I should have bet on black.

MINE OFFENSES

BY R. J. JOSEPH

Hated my mouth. Full, thick, juicy lips,
forming a multitude of words
bubbling up through the orifice, oozing from my soul.
Daddy never wanted to hear anything I had to say.
Mama had to always work.
The mouth offended—
I sliced the lips off, severed their hold on the words.

Hated my breasts. Pre-pubescent,
barely budded yet capturing
the attention of boys and grown men alike.
Classmates grabbed them, swatting and bruising.
The bus driver pinched them.
The breasts offended—
I seared them away, burned flesh stank ugly to all.

Hated my vagina. Sticky and slick even when
I didn't know why, calling to men I didn't like
and crying when they forced inside.
The men didn't ask permission or care about the pain.
They plundered and I shrank.
The vagina offended—
I sewed it shut, brown welcome mat open no more.

Hated my brain. Full with vestiges of revenge.
Materializing solutions where there were none.
Aching to disappear into nothing.
No one would miss my thoughts.
No one heard me.
The brain offended—
I bashed it out, congealed matter running from knowing.

Loved my rebirth. Powerful.
Reeking of decay. Triumphant in shedding
the obstacle of tortured life.
They would all listen now, to my unspoken words.
They would recognize.
They had offended—
I will hunt them. Slicing and searing, sewing and bashing
    forever.

THERE IS NO DIFFERENCE BETWEEN AN EYE AND A MOUTH

BY DONYAE COLES

I.

The ceiling split, an eye—a mouth, void but full, so full
a plaster sky, rent in two
the land of her thighs split open
on her wedding night she lay feverish, hot, open
"Stress, jitters, change in weather," the aunties whispered
and above it whispered—
rolling, twisting darkness, sparkling wet and alive,
black diamonds just beyond her husband's back
promises.

II.

It came with the fever—that terrible mouth
split open plaster like flesh and whispered—the more delirious the
    better
promises,
it had been promised—sweat slick, she needed that pitch dark just
    beyond her fingers

that violent soft shadow, that slimy, crushing void all alive with
    itself, an open mouth, an open eye
seen, felt it closer as the fevers ran higher and higher—her heat a
    prayer to that black heaven
she learned how to bring them—howls to winter moons, mad rain
    dances, herbs from old, dry books
and it sang above her yes, yes, yes in words that were not chants to
    her moans—
her husband watched from the door—didn't know what he saw.

III.

A mouth could be entered—she could enter
sure, so sure, she laid in twisting sheets
her body dripping, fading, aching close—so close but not enough,
    never enough until—
it was and she was gone—finally—the space beyond
close enough to sink trembling fingers into—hot and alive,
    crushing, sucking, taking
she wanted to ask, there had been a promise but—oh oh oh—
she was black stars, diamonds, dust gone.

IV.

"She was always weak," the aunties said
as they consoled her husband and showed him a new wife—a good
    girl, a godly girl—
the eye—for them an eye, only an eye—watched on and waited for
    another fever.

NOTES FOR MY SISTERS WHEN I AM GONE

BY PATRICIA LILLIE

They think their Happy Ever After depends upon our deaths.

Do not accept
a first-born child as reckoning
for your lettuce.

They love the chamomile, the lavender, the sage, but not so much the
     oleander, the foxglove, or the yew.
And yet they'll take the apple when it's offered.

Wandering children will
eat you out of
house and home.
Siblings are the worst.

They'll ask for brews and philters, straw spun into gold and ointments
     for the clap, but they control the story. Even if the prince turns out
     to be a frog.
Especially if the prince turns out to be a frog.

Never trust a juniper tree
or the song the
red bird sings.

In the end, they'll call you crone and hag and bitch. They'll come with
fire and stones and hangman's hemp.
They'll make you dance in red-hot shoes.

Their
Happy Ever After
depends upon
your death.

LOW TIDE

BY SARAH READ

Sand down her throat like an hourglass
Measuring the minutes
In a riptide.

When the waves come
She streams in,
Suit-less.

A density of heart
Like ballast
Overthrown.

WANING MOON

BY ALICIA HILTON

Whenever the moon wanes from sphere to sickle
pieces of me fracture scatter teeth jawbone femurs

Even toes snap off gnarled the bunions just like
my dead mother's toes loss linked with love

Heaven knows why I fall apart doctors could
not explain or cure my disintegrating cartilage

The first time it happened a nurse called a priest
he was perplexed the hospital reeked of antiseptic

An orderly swept pieces of me into a dustbin
the poor man screeched when the broom flew

From his hand shattered the window ghosts are
not supposed to be real but I heard my mother

Singing her favorite song Moon River I smelled
her perfume bergamot incense she pieced me together

Like a jigsaw her warm hand grasped my shoulder
scapula connected to clavicle humerus linked with

Radius my teeth flew back into my mouth don't cry
she whispered her apparition materialized beside

The shattered window united we floated into the night
now when the moon wanes Mother waits beside me

Water swirls around our boat two drifters we row
toward the end of the world she drops her oars

Grasps my hand gently so gently rain begins to fall
a heron calls to her daughter the grey birds fly

Toward heaven lightning streaks across the sky
I feel my bones coming apart but I smile

SKINWALKER MOON

BY BRENDA S. TOLIAN

wolfskin, dry crackle, ragged fur
i taste you on the western wind
tension, four limbed, two feet, two hands
below the peaceful pinyon, the sun has gone to blood
dripping down the Sangre de Cristo—*i need you*

gravel in my belly, hunger, mastication
claws grip the edge of the caldera
salt -sweat, and fear rolling over my tongue
howling to answering coyotes
the hunt, leaping over prickly pear
running until my chest bursts
i want you—*in my throat*

blade on belly, ragged teeth, count of twenty
slip skin, wet fabric, knitted cells
pulling the edges of your smiling meat mask
slow, warm, wet
neck, chin, and lip—*i become you*

drums, flickering pulse between sweat lined thighs
broken breastbone, cracking ribs, pull them wide
blood of sacred eagle

wings erect, you breathe through them
shake out of your skin, unzip your vertebrae
shiver, fine hair still erect
obsidian blade, peel away—*what i need*

slip into your body to become
breast of moon exhales over the dunes
warm and heavy your wet skin
claws sharpened on twisted cottonwood
my tongue licks your blood-flecked lips
elk white skull bone on my head
there is magic in the night
your muscle in my mouth
your warm heart in my hands
i am you
the you—*that i never had*

WHAT MONSTER IS THIS

BY INGRID L. TAYLOR

You made me voyeur
in my own castle, a pomegranate mouth
edged with cosmos & wrongly built,
to keen for the slip of your heart
peeled from your ribcage shell.
Do not forgive me because I want
the same as you—to break
on our bodies' borders, to pass through
the skin & everything beneath,
for the caress and the silver delight
that binds one to another's flesh.

You called me to storm,
& I chose the lightning
freak of sky
that splits to make me
whole. What monster is this
rare body of dissonant notes
rising to fuck & imbibe unrepentant,
whose rampage will cut
a bloodied swath across your velvet
silk & bone. I am atmosphere
sheltered in birdsong,
I nest in the waft of morning
& a sun that embraces the tender parts
you would not touch.
I enter this world you cast
to a mockingbird's tune
open my mouth
and sing.

ON DARKEST NIGHT OF FAERIE BRIGHT

BY SUMIKO SAULSON

In an anxious child's maw wiggles a single tooth
When he bites on a carrot, it comes hastily loose
Sell it off late at night for the price of two quarters
To the grim faeries famously known as tooth hoarders

Ignorant parents open windowpanes wide
To invite all the night's hungry faeries inside
Little thieves glimmer bright stealing teeth in the night
Shining like fireflies in the low firelight

Faerie flight enters tiny, aloft glowing sprite
But they stretch and they grow to an enormous height
Talon-like fingerclaws drag on the ground
On the floorboards they scrape, such a nail-biting sound
Sunken eyes of deep red glowing like a hellhound

Rows of sharp shark-like fangs gracing sardonic grin
Three-inch denticles stretching from nostril to chin
These can easily slice through a soft human's skin
How the bright faerie drools, all its hunger to sate

Inhaled lovely aromas arouse its palate
For the teeth of a child aren't its only cuisine
Nor the only ones that it enjoys loosening

Upstairs yon tot's grandmother restlessly sleeps
In her nightmares preparing, she quietly weeps
For a long finger prying most gently in mouth
As it loosens her teeth to the north, east and south
It inhales her last breath 'til there's nothing to save
For she won't need to take all her teeth to the grave

When the morning arrives, see her grizzly demise
Cold coins lying on each of her dead, sunken eyes

MOON

BY CORRINE DE WINTER

Yes, I share my light.
I spread legend and myth among you,
But I care not what you think.
The psychology of my fullness
Gives you pause, warps you
As I outshine everything in your path.
While you are earthbound this victory will not end.
You speak of my countenance,
Create names for my scars,
Silly human titles.
You call me Moon,
But I am so much more.
I am the ultimate brilliance in 12 parts,
And you will always, always, always
Be beneath me.

FERRYWOMAN OF GEOJE-DO

BY PATRICIA FLAHERTY PAGAN

Tiny Furies
Ankle-grabbers on the gray pebble beach,
climbing
lying in wait in the pocket of my snug black parka.

Tree Street is Sunday-morning silent
Daiso's doors gape open
plush yellow smiley face pillows, PEEP-yellow
beckon from the corner

Consume me.

Three sets of knife-edged canines
sink into my soft middle,
Ferrywoman, to carry, not to judge.

I catch snatches of Norwegian, French, Busan slang,
blade of a carrot peeler glints
treasure for 2,000 won.

Megaera hisses at her sisters-

I bump shoulders with their prey,
gaunt, blue-eyed engineer,
at the shiny elevator doors
and the bitter sisters alight.

Rubbing a smooth, red hair ribbon
wrapping my expatriate solitude around me, a nubby scarf
hearing his screams as curses attack.

Fluent in vengeance.

BRIGHT TAPESTRY

BY CARINA BISSETT

The solitary woman stalks alleys,
a time traveler spinning dark
matter, the cosmic web.
She searches for eyeshine,
animal bridegrooms disguised
as bluebeards, princes, and wolves.
The cherry burns. Cigarette smoke
tangles. City sewers steam.
The flash of teeth cut, sword shining,
and Penelope grins, ash swept under stiletto.
The hunt begins—again.

Tapetum lucidum
—the scientific term
unravels the weave illuminating
nights when cunning suitors roam.
Lust incarnate, a matrix lurking,
retroflection faceted, opalescent rainbow
cast. An optical illusion.

In Ithaca, Sparta's daughter unravels
the day's work dismantled,
purity apparent, pedestal shrouded
in myth and magic and myrrh.

The wanderer's wife toils, invisible,
silence shuttled in a song of carnage,
a panacea. Victory branches,
the iridescent naiad, Mother of Pearl,
mineraloid multiplied, unraveled.
The weaver, the woman, silenced.
And Nobody's eyes needle open.

Forewarned, Penelope walks, spindle raised,
prepared to slay monsters and men.
She strings her loom with gut
weighted down with severed heads
whispering tales, taut, warnings bound
in warp and weft spun on the distaff side
      —a bright tapestry.

NECROW

BY QUERUS ABUTTU

Snip, flash, grind and gash—
Beaks bloom red on Mommy's head.
The murder hops as her corpse drops.
Feathers worm into the dead.

Undulating. Fornicating.
Between the thighs, a Corvid sighs.
Rigor sweet. A nascent treat.
Mother's belly starts to rise.

Tearing. Shredding.
Bursting black. Anemic moon of light.
Ghastly cry. Crazed lullaby.
Wings unfurl and slice the night.

ON THE ALTAR OF A BESEECHING BELL, WOEBEGONE WITH CAPTIVITY

BY SABA SYED RAZVI

O nightfire thrum, this Wolf Moon is rust and blood, is
breathless bone and clay on the mindless mind.
Beside the glimmer of the comet come once
a thousand years, the moon is howling back
at my light spilling from wailing mouth,
a waxen memory.
This Wolf Moon is magma and black sand, is
lusting for the taste of salt sweat and gristle,
bearing iridescent shimmer in the twilight.
But the cards speak of a Druidess, tentacled
and terrifying. A Coming. She calls upon the moss
to blot with softness my bleeding feet,
drink their tenor, the Black Forest wine of their path

This Wolf Moon is nothing of cherry sweetness, is
just smoky in its harshening, is
the abyss grown wide.
By the runes, carved in roughest stone, the ink
sings its own woes.
What tale of hopeless, heedless stunning
will be, now divined?
This Wolf Moon is blood and rust on a blade,
leaving the bone and clay breathless, mind.
Strike the beast moon from its orbit, and swallow it
like a candy pearl; be the wolf that inhabits your waning;
be still in your space,
your ritual—an invocation
for the howling in our blood, a wanderlust
born for a lupine longing so much more than predatory.

ORCHID MOON

BY LEE MURRAY

while you sleep
Little Wife
cuts wet halfmoons
into your open palms

like curved beaks
they clamour
skylark syllables of despair
dark with putrid breath

while you sleep
fingers domed as a teak cage
you clasp at tumours
bloat-bellied with pustulating spite

as half-white tendrils
of an unquiet spirit
snake bitter through your bones
you slumber, still

and outside
on the greasy stoop
Little Wife
flirts with an orchid moon

ABOUT THE EDITOR

Stephanie M. Wytovich is an American poet, novelist, and essayist. Her work has been showcased in numerous venues such as *Weird Tales*, *Nightmare Magazine*, *Year's Best Hardcore Horror: Volume 2*, *The Best Horror of the Year: Volume 8*, as well as many others.

Wytovich is the Poetry Editor for Raw Dog Screaming Press, an adjunct at Western Connecticut State University, Southern New Hampshire University, and Point Park University, and a mentor with Crystal Lake Publishing. She is a member of the Science Fiction Poetry Association, an active member of the Horror Writers Association, and a graduate of Seton Hill University's MFA program for Writing Popular Fiction. Her Bram Stoker Award-winning poetry collection, *Brothel*, earned a home with Raw Dog Screaming Press alongside *Hysteria: A Collection of Madness*, *Mourning Jewelry*, *An Exorcism of Angels*, *Sheet Music to My Acoustic Nightmare*, and most recently, *The Apocalyptic Mannequin*. Her debut novel, *The Eighth*, is published with Dark Regions Press.

Follow Wytovich on her blog at http://stephaniewytovich.blogspot.com/ and on Twitter @SWytovich.

ABOUT THE JUDGES

Angela Yuriko Smith is an American poet, author, and publisher with over 20 years of experience in newspaper journalism. She is a Bram Stoker Awards® Finalist and HWA Mentor of the Year for 2020. She publishes *Space and Time*, a publication dedicated to fantasy, horror, and science fiction since 1966. Visit Angela at angelayurikosmith.com.

Sara Tantlinger is the author of the Bram Stoker Award-winning *The Devil's Dreamland: Poetry Inspired by H.H. Holmes,* and the Stoker-nominated works *To Be Devoured, Cradleland of Parasites,* and *Not All Monsters.* Along with being a mentor for the HWA Mentorship Program, she is also a co-organizer for the HWA Pittsburgh Chapter. She embraces all things macabre and can be found lurking in graveyards or on Twitter @SaraTantlinger, at saratantlinger.com and on Instagram @inkychaotics.

ABOUT THE POETS

Querus Abuttu or "Dr. Q.," is the creator of the Iron Shores world. She writes strange dark tales, relevant speculative fiction, and science-based sci-fi. She is also a poet, savior of road turtles, and a solitary green-gray witch of the hills. When she's not writing, Dr. Q. explores the wilds of Virginia and interviews interesting individuals for her next novel. She loves foraging for wild foods, gardening, and trying to find 101 ways to thwart deer from eating her plants. You may find her in a local pub drinking craft beers, talking to random people, and writing furiously in a tattered notebook that she keeps under her pillow at night. Visit her author website at QuerusAbuttu.com and discover her work on her Amazon author page https://www.amazon.com/Querus-Abuttu/e/B009NDJ2RM.

Michael Arnzen holds four Bram Stoker Awards® and an International Horror Guild Award for his disturbing (and often funny) poetry, fiction, and literary experiments. He has been teaching as a Professor of English in the MFA program in Writing Popular Fiction at Seton Hill University since 1999. To learn more about his writing, seek out the books *Proverbs for Monsters* or *100 Jolts*, which collect the best of it to date. To see what he's up to now, visit gorelets.com or follow him on twitter @MikeArnzen where he routinely posts news, oddities, and random tidbits of terror.

Carina Bissett is a writer, poet, and educator working primarily in the fields of dark fiction and fabulism. Her short fiction and poetry have been published in multiple journals and anthologies including *Upon a Twice Time, Bitter Distillations: An Anthology of Poisonous Tales, Arterial Bloom, Gorgon: Stories of Emergence, Hath No Fury*, and the *HWA Poetry Showcase Vol. V* and *VI*. She is also the co-editor of *Shadow Atlas: Dark Landscapes of the Americas*. Links to her work can be found at http://carinabissett.com.

Manny Blacksher has spent long periods in Montreal and Dublin, but he's back now where he began in the heart of Alabama's Southern Gothic—Mobile. He's published over seventy-five poems in US and international literary publications, along with a handful of peculiar short stories. He's particularly grateful to have been awarded HWA's 2020 Dark Poetry Scholarship.

Robert Payne Cabeen is a screenwriter, artist, purveyor of narrative horror poetry, and now a novelist, with his Bram Stoker Award-winning debut *Cold Cuts*, from Omnium Gatherum. His screenwriting credits include *Heavy Metal 2000* for Columbia TriStar, Sony Pictures, *A Monkey's Tale,* and *Walking with Buddha.* Cabeen's illustrated book, *Fearworms: Selected Poems,* was a Bram Stoker Award nominee. As creative director for Streamline Pictures, Robert helped anime pioneer Carl Macek bring Japanese animated features, like *Akira* and dozens of other classics, to a western audience. Cabeen received a Master of Fine Arts degree from Otis Art Institute, with a dual major in painting and design. Since then, he has combined his interests in the visual arts with screenwriting and storytelling for a broad range of entertainment companies including Warner Brothers, Columbia/TriStar, Disney, Sony, Universal, USA Network, Nelvana, and SEGA. For more about Robert Payne Cabeen, visit: robertpaynecabeen.com.

Brad P. Christy is an award-winning author of a dozen published short stories and poetry. He was the runner-up in the Writer's League of Texas 2021 worldwide manuscript competition and was an honorable mention in the 2021 (3rd quarter) L. Ron Hubbard Writers of the Future Contest for science fiction. He is a member of the Horror Writers Association and the Writer's League of Texas and holds a master's degree in Creative Writing and English. As an English teacher, he devotes time to volunteering as a writing coach. As a sucker, he volunteers to transport rescue animals and has a long history of adopting stray cats. Brad currently lives in Central Texas with his wife ... and far too many cats.

Donyae Coles is a writer of weird and horror fiction. Her debut novel is releasing in 2022. You can find more of her publications at www.donyaecoles.com and follow her on Twitter @okokno, she's delightful.

Deborah L. Davitt was raised in Nevada, but currently lives in Houston, Texas with her husband and son. Her poetry has received Rhysling, Dwarf Star, and Pushcart nominations and has appeared in over fifty journals, including *F&SF* and *Asimov's Science Fiction*. Her short fiction has appeared in *Analog* and *Galaxy's Edge*. For more about her work, including her novels, short stories, and her Elgin-nominated poetry collection, *The Gates of Never,* please see www.edda-earth.com.

Corrine De Winter is an author and Stoker Award Winner for her poetry collection "The Women at the Funeral." De Winter has won numerous awards for her writing from the New York Quarterly, Triton College of Arts & Sciences, and The Rhysling Science Fiction Award. Her work has been applauded by such luminaries as William Peter Blatty (*The Exorcist* author), Tom Monteleone, Thomas Ligotti, Nick Cave, Stanley Wiater, Heather Graham, and others.

Stephanie Ellis writes dark speculative prose and poetry and has been published in a variety of magazines and anthologies, including Off Limits Press' *Far From Home*, Silver Shamrock's *Midnight in the Pentagram*, and she will also feature in the upcoming *Were Tales* from Brigids Gate Press, Demain Publishing's *A Silent Dystopia*, and Silver Shamrock's *Midnight from Beyond the Stars*. Her poetry has been published in the *HWA Poetry Showcase Volumes VI and VII* as well as in the collections, *The Art of Dying* and *Dark is my Playground*; her dark nursery rhymes are to be found in *One, Two, I See You*. Longer work includes the folk horror novel, *The Five Turns of the Wheel* and the gothic novella, *Bottled,* both published by Silver Shamrock. Her new short story collection, *As the Wheel Turns—More Tales from the Weald* features stories set in the world of the Five Turns. She is co-editor of Trembling with Fear, HorrorTree.com's online magazine and also co-editor at the female-centric, Black Angel Press, producing the *Daughters of Darkness* anthologies. She is an active member of the HWA and can be found at https://stephanieellis.org and on twitter at @el_stevie.

Jeannine Hall Gailey is a poet with MS who served as the second Poet Laureate of Redmond, Washington. She's the author of five books of poetry: *Becoming the Villainess, She Returns to the Floating World, Unexplained Fevers, The Robot Scientist's Daughter*, and *Field Guide to the End of the World*, winner of the Moon City Press Book Prize and the SFPA's Elgin Award. Her work appeared in journals like *The American Poetry Review, Ploughshares,* and *Poetry*. Her web site is www.webbish6.com. Twitter and Instagram: @webbish6.

Emma J. Gibbon is originally from Yorkshire in the U.K. and now lives in Midcoast Maine. She is a horror writer and Rhysling-nominated speculative poet. Her debut fiction collection, *Dark Blood Comes from the Feet*, from Trepidatio Publishing, was one of NPR's best books of 2020, and won the Maine Literary Book Award for Speculative Fiction. Her stories have appeared in The Dark Tome, and Toasted Cake podcasts, and the anthologies, *The Muse & The Flame, Wicked Haunted*, and *Wicked Weird*. Her poetry has been published in *Strange Horizons, Liminality, Pedestal Magazine,* and *Kaleidotrope*. Emma lives with her husband, Steve, and three exceptional animals: Odin, Mothra, and M. Bison (also known as Grim) in a spooky little house in the woods. She is a member of the Horror Writers Association, the New England Horror Writers, and the Science Fiction & Fantasy Poetry Association.

Currently in her second-term as Poet Laureate of New Bedford,

Massachusetts, author and playwright **Patricia Gomes** is the former editor of *Adagio Verse Quarterly*, and has been published in numerous literary journals and anthologies, including New England Horror Writers anthology *Wicked Women*. A 2018 and 2008 Pushcart Prize nominee, and twice nominated for a Rhysling Science Fiction award, Gomes is the author of four chapbooks. Ms. Gomes' recent publications include *Tidings, Star*Line, Muddy River Review, Rituals, Sledgehammer*, and *Apex and Abyss*. Ms. Gomes is the co-founder of the GNB Writers Block as well a member of the SciFi Poetry Association, New England Horror Writers, the Horror Writers Association, and the Massachusetts Poetry Society.

Kerri-Leigh Grady is a writer, a software developer, a middling woodworker, a terrible metalsmith, a lover of tea, and generally up to no good in Seattle.

KC Grifant is a New England-to-SoCal transplant who writes internationally published horror, fantasy, science fiction, and weird western stories for collectible card games, podcasts, anthologies, and magazines. Her writings have appeared in *Andromeda Spaceways Magazine, Aurealis Magazine, Mythaxis Magazine, Unnerving Magazine, Frozen Wavelets, The Lovecraft eZine, Colp Magazine*, and others. Her short stories have haunted dozens of collections, including *We Shall Be Monsters; Shadowy Natures: Tales of Psychological Horror; The One That Got Away: Women of Horror Anthology Volume 3; Beyond the Infinite: Tales from the Outer Reaches; Six Guns Straight From Hell Volume 3*; and the Stoker-nominated *Fright Mare: Women Write Horror*. In addition, she co-founded the San Diego HWA chapter in 2016. Aside from writing speculative fiction, KC is an award-winning science writer, editor, and communications professional who has written hundreds of nonfiction articles and feature stories. In her spare time, she consumes too much coffee and chases a wild toddler. For more information, visit www.KCGrifant.com or connect on social media via @kcgrifant.

Amanda Hard holds an MFA in Creative Writing from Murray State University. She is a member of the Codex Writer's Group and the Science Fiction and Fantasy Poetry Association. Her poetry and short stories have appeared in *Lamplight*, *MetaStellar*, *parAbnormal*, and other magazines and anthologies. A former print journalist and science writer, she lives in the cornfields of southern Indiana.

Chad Helder is the author of *The Dead Mall Horror: A Novel in 49 Poems*, *Pop-Up Book of Death*, and *The Vampire Bridegroom*. With Vince Liaguno, Helder co-edited *Unspeakable Horror: From the Shadows of the Closet*, a queer horror anthology, which won the Bram Stoker Award for Superior Achievement in an Anthology.

Jamal Hodge is a multi-award-winning film director and writer. He is an active member of the HWA and the SFPA, being nominated for a 2021 Rhysling Award for his Poem "Fermi's Spaceship". His screenplay "Mourning Meal" has won 5 awards (including best short screenplay at the NYC Horror Film Festival 2018). He is currently devising devious worlds to be explored in his first novel and poetry collection.

Alicia Hilton is an author, arbitrator, law professor, actor, and former FBI Special Agent. She believes in angels and demons, magic, and monsters. Her work has appeared in *Akashic Books, Best Indie Speculative Fiction Volume 3, Cemetery Gates Media, Daily Science Fiction, Demain Publishing UK, DreamForge, Dreams & Nightmares, Litro, Modern Haiku, Sci Phi Journal, Space and Time, Spectral Realms, Vastarien, Year's Best Hardcore Horror Volumes 4, 5, & 6*, and elsewhere. Alicia is a member of HWA, SFPA, and SFWA. Her website is https://aliciahilton.com. Follow her on Twitter @aliciahilton01.

Ian Hunter was born in Edinburgh, Scotland and is a member of the UK Chapter of the Horror Writers Association, and the Glasgow SF Writers Circle. He has been a member of the British Fantasy Society for over thirty years and their poetry editor for over ten years. His poems have appeared in *Star*Line, Dreams and Nightmares, Dark Horizons, New Writing Scotland, Nasty Piece of Work, Dreich*, and many other magazines and anthologies in the UK, USA, and Canada. He has twice been a writer in residence and also writes children's novels, short stories, and occasionally edits anthologies and small press magazines, as well as often reviewing for a variety of outlets. He is really chuffed to be included here.

Benicio Isandro is a writer and poet with a penchant for all things macabre, paranormal, esoteric, and weird. By day, Beni haunts the bloody lab benches of medical labs. By night, he writes speculative flash fiction, haiku, haibun, and web code. His work can be found in *Drifting Sands Haibun, The Nottingham Horror Collective,* and other publications. Find him at www.benicioisandro.com.

R. J. Joseph is a Bram Stoker Award®-nominated, Texas based writer who earned her MFA in Writing Popular Fiction from Seton Hill University. When she isn't writing, reading, or teaching, she can usually be found wrangling her huge, blended family of one husband, four adult sprouts, seven teenaged sproutlings, four grandboo seedlings, and one furry hellbeast who sometimes pretends to be a dog. She occasionally peeks out on Twitter @rjacksonjoseph or on Amazon at: https://amzn.to/3igvz67.

Naching T. Kassa is a wife, mother, and horror writer. She's created short stories, novellas, poems, and co-created three children. She lives in Eastern Washington State with her husband, Dan Kassa. Naching is a member of the Horror Writers Association, Head of Publishing and Interviewer for HorrorAddicts.net, and an assistant and staff writer for *Still Water Bay* at Crystal Lake Publishing.

Lorna Dickson Keach (she/her) isn't haunted, but she does read and write about haunted things. She graduated from the University of Nevada, Las Vegas with a degree in English, and she tweets @LornaDKeach. More of her work may be found at lornakeach.com.

Once upon a time, **Katherine Kerestman** had earned B.A. in History & English from John Carroll University, and an M.A. in English from Case Western Reserve University and had embarked upon further studies in English—when a bite of an apple poisoned with pragmatism brought about a career shift which, in effect, strangled her artistic soul. Longing to romp in gothic ruins, crumbling castles, and claustrophobic Puritan and Shirley Jackson-esque villages, she began to write down her dreams, and suddenly they took wing as stories. She spent the next year writing her first book—*Creepy Cat's Macabre Travels: Prowling around Haunted Towers, Crumbling Castles, and Ghoulish Graveyard*, a nonfiction literary- and historically-oriented travel memoir that placed on the Preliminary Ballot for the 2020 Bram Stoker Awards, in the nonfiction category. She has also published a short story called "Markovia" in S. T. Joshi's *Penumbra* No. 2 (July 2021); "Breaking the Shackles of the Great Chain of Being and Liberating Compassion in the Eighteenth Century" in the journal *1650-1850: Ideas, Aesthetics, and Inquiries in the Early Modern Era;* and various movie and book reviews in forums such as *Buddy Hollywood* (online blog) and *Voices* (the newsletter for the Dracula Society). Additional works have been accepted for publication in the near future. She is a member of the Jane Austen Society of North America, Mensa, the Horror Writers Association, and the Dracula Society, and is active in the *Dark Shadows* fandom. You can find her frolicking in the cemeteries of Salem most Halloween nights.

EV Knight is the author of the Stoker-winning debut novel *The Fourth Whore*. She has also written a novella titled *Dead Eyes* for Unnerving Press's Rewind or Die series. EV's second novel *Children of Demeter* will be released August 2021. Her short stories and poetry can be found in a number of anthologies, magazines, and the HWA's 2019 *Poetry Showcase*. She received her MFA in Writing Creative Fiction from Seton Hill University in 2019. A lover of all things dark and creepy, EV can be found wandering the haunted streets of Savannah, Georgia with her husband Matt, and their three naughty sphynx cats—Feenix, Bizzabout Fitchett, and Ozymandias Fuzzfoot the First.

Amy Langevin is a poet and student at LACC. Her writing explores mental illness, fictional serial murder, and transformation. While bored at work, she wrote her first collection *The Man Who Married Death*, a story of a man's descent into madness and serial murder told through poetry. Former versions of her poems "My Dear Mother," "Ruby Splashes," "Thirst," "The Better Half," and "To My Beloved Dead Wife" were published in horror anthology *Into the Night* (Dark Night Publishing). She is a supporting member of the HWA. Visit her at www.amylangevinterrormirror.wordpress.com.

Beverley Lee is the bestselling author of the Gabriel Davenport series *(The Making of Gabriel Davenport, A Shining in the Shadows*, and *The Purity of Crimson), The Ruin of Delicate Things,* and *The House of Little Bones (September 2021).* Her shorter fiction has been included in works from Cemetery Gates Media, Kandisha Press, and Off Limits Press. In thrall to the written word from an early age, especially the darker side of fiction, she believes that the very best story is the one you have to tell. Supporting fellow authors is also her passion and she is actively involved in social media and writers' groups. You can visit her online at www.beverleylee.com (where you'll find a free dark and twisted short story download) or on Instagram (@theconstantvoice) and Twitter (@constantvoice).

Vince A. Liaguno is a healthcare administrator by day, writer, editor/anthologist, and pop culture enthusiast by night, whose jam is books, slasher films, and Jamie Lee Curtis. He is the Bram Stoker Award-winning editor of *Unspeakable Horror: From the Shadows of the Closet* (Dark Scribe Press, 2008), *Butcher Knives & Body Counts: Essays of the Formula, Frights, and Fun of the Slasher Film* (Dark Scribe Press, 2011), *Unspeakable Horror 2: Abominations of Desire* (Evil Jester Press, 2017), and the upcoming *Other Terrors: An Inclusive Anthology* (Houghton Mifflin Harcourt, 2022). Visit him online at: www.VinceLiaguno.com.

Patricia Lillie grew up in a haunted house in a small town in Northeast Ohio. Since then, she has published picture books, short stories, fonts, and two novels. Her latest, *The Cuckoo Girls*, was a 2020 Bram Stoker Award® finalist in the category of Fiction Collection. As Patricia Lillie, she is the author of *The Ceiling Man*, a novel of quiet horror, and as Kay Charles, the author of *Ghosts in Glass Houses*, a cozy-ish mystery with ghosts. She is a graduate of Parsons School of Design, has an MFA in Writing Popular Fiction from Seton Hill University, and teaches in Southern New Hampshire University's MFA program. She also knits and sometimes purls.

Donna Lynch is horror and dark fiction author, singer, lyricist, spoken word artist, and two-time Bram Stoker Award-nominated poet. She has published seven poetry collections, as well as novels and a novella. She and her husband, artist and musician Steven Archer, are the founding members of the dark rock band Ego Likeness (Metropolis Records). They live in Maryland.

Caitlin Marceau is an author and lecturer living and working in Montreal. She holds a B.A. in Creative Writing, is a member of both the Horror Writers Association and the Quebec Writers' Federation, and spends most of her time writing horror and experimental fiction. She's been published for journalism, poetry, as well as creative non-fiction, and has spoken about horror literature at several Canadian conventions. Her collections, *A Blackness Absolute* and *Palimpsest*, are slated for publication by D&T Publishing LLC and Ghost Orchid Press in 2022 respectively. If she's not covered in ink or wading through stacks of paper, you can find her ranting about issues in pop culture or nerding out over a good book. For more, check out CaitlinMarceau.ca.

Graham Masterton is mainly recognized for his horror novels, but he has also been a prolific writer of thrillers, disaster novels, and historical epics, as well as one of the world's most influential series of sex instruction books. He became a newspaper reporter at the age of 17 and was appointed editor of *Penthouse* magazine at only 24. His first horror novel *The Manitou* was filmed with Tony Curtis playing the lead, and three of his short horror stories were filmed by Tony Scott for *The Hunger* TV series. Ten years ago, Graham turned his hand to crime novels and *White Bones*, set in Ireland, was followed by ten more bestselling crime novels featuring Detective Superintendent Katie Maguire, the latest of which is *The Last Drop of Blood*. In 2019 he was given a Lifetime Achievement Award by the Horror Writers Association. A new horror novel *The Shadow People* will be published in 2021, to be followed by *The Soul Stealer* in 2022. He is a frequent visitor to Poland where *The Manitou* was the first Western horror novel published after the fall of Communism and *How To Drive Your Man Wild In Bed (Magia Seksu)* was the first non-medical sex advice book. He has established an award for short stories written by inmates in Polish prisons, *Nagroda Grahama Mastertona "W Więzieniu Pisane"* to be presented for the fifth time this year. A bronze Graham Masterton gnome has recently been added to the tourist attractions in the streets of Wrocław. He is currently working on new horror novels and is co-writing a series of new horror stories with Dawn G. Harris.

Lisa Morton is a screenwriter, author of non-fiction books, and award-winning prose writer whose work was described by the American Library Association's *Readers' Advisory Guide to Horror* as "consistently dark, unsettling, and frightening". She is the author of four novels and 150 short stories, a six-time winner of the Bram Stoker Award®, and a world-class Halloween expert. Her most recent books are the anthology *Weird Women 2: Classic Supernatural Fiction by Groundbreaking Female Writers* (co-edited with Leslie S. Klinger) and the collection *Night Terrors & Other Tales,* and her original weekly fiction podcast *Spine Tinglers* recently debuted. This is her fourth appearance in HWA's *Poetry Showcase* series. Lisa lives in the San Fernando Valley and online at www.lisamorton.com.

Lee Murray is a multi-award-winning author-editor and poet from Aotearoa-New Zealand (Sir Julius Vogel, Australian Shadows) and a double Bram Stoker Award® winner. A NZSA Honorary Literary Fellow, Lee is the Grimshaw Sargeson Fellow for 2021 for her narrative prose-poetry work *Fox Spirit on a Distant Cloud*. Her debut poetry collection, *Tortured Willows*, a collaboration with Christina Sng, Angela Yuriko Smith, and Geneve Flynn, is forthcoming from Yuriko Publishing. Read more at leemurray.info.

Ronald J. Murray is a writer of speculative fiction and poetry living in Pittsburgh, Pennsylvania. His published work includes his two dark poetry collections, *Cries to Kill the Corpse Flower* and *Lost Letters to a Lover's Carcass*. His short fiction and poetry has appeared in *Space and Time Magazine*, on The Wicked Library Podcast, in *Bon Appetit: Stories and Recipes for Human Consumption*, the forthcoming anthology from Infernal Ink Books, *Lustcraftian Horrors: Erotic Stories Inspired by H.P. Lovecraft*, and more.

Lonnie Nadler is a writer from Vancouver, Canada. He released his critically acclaimed debut graphic novel, *The Dregs*, in 2017 from Black Mask Studios. His 2018 follow-up, *Come Into Me*, was named one of the best 100 horror comics of all time by *Paste Magazine*. In 2020, his historical folk horror book, *Black Stars Above*, made the Preliminary Ballot for the Bram Stoker Awards. Lonnie has also penned stories for Marvel Comics, Aftershock Comics, VICE, Blood-Disgusting, and numerous other publications.

Patricia Flaherty Pagan was born in Boston and has lived in four countries. She is the author of *Trail Ways Pilgrims: Stories* and *Enduring Spirit: Stories*. In addition to writing award-winning literary, horror, fantasy, and crime short stories and poems, she has edited several collections of fiction and poetry by women writers. She teaches workshops about writing complex, female-identifying characters. Learn more about her at www.patriciaflahertypagan.com.

Cynthia Pelayo is a two-time Bram Stoker Award-nominated author and poet. She lives in Chicago with her family.

Saba Syed Razvi, PhD is the author of the Elgin Award-nominated collection *In the Crocodile Gardens* (Agape Editions) and the collection *heliophobia* (Finishing Line Press), which appeared on the preliminary ballot for the Bram Stoker Award ® for Superior Achievement in Poetry, as well as the chapbooks *Limerence & Lux* (Chax Press), *Of the Divining and the Dead* (Finishing Line Press), and *Beside the Muezzin's Call & Beyond the Harem's Veil* (Finishing Line Press). She is currently an Associate Professor of English and Creative Writing at the University of Houston in Victoria, TX, where in addition to working on scholarly research on interfaces between contemporary poetry and science and on gender & sexuality in speculative and horror literature and pop-culture, she is writing new poems and fiction.

Sarah Read is a dark fiction writer in the frozen north of Wisconsin. Her short stories can be found in various places, including Ellen Datlow's *Best Horror of the Year* vols 10 and 12. Her short fiction collection *Out of Water* is available from Trepidatio Publishing, as is her debut novel *The Bone Weaver's Orchard*, both nominated for the Bram Stoker, This is Horror, and Ladies of Horror Fiction Awards. *Orchard* won the Stoker for Superior Achievement in a First Novel and the This Is Horror Award for Novel of the Year. *Orchard* is also available in Spanish under the title *El Jardin Del Tallador De Huesos*, published by Dilatande Mentes, where it has been nominated for the Guillermo de Baskerville Award. When she's not staring into the abyss, she knits. You can find her online on Instagram or Twitter @inkwellmonster or on her site at www.inkwellmonster.wordpress.com.

Terrie Leigh Relf is an active member of HWA and a Lifetime Member of the SFPA. She is the poetry editor for *Tales from the Moonlit Path* and is on staff at Hiraeth Publishing, where she is the contest judge/editor for the quarterly drabble contest, the lead editor for *Hungur Chronicles,* and serves on various special projects. In addition to being a writer and editor, Relf is also a life and writing coach. You can learn more about her endeavors at https://tlrelf.wordpress.com/, https://tlrelfreikipractitioner.wordpress.com/about/, and https://terrieleighrelf.com/.

Lindy Ryan is an award-winning horror and dark fantasy editor and author. Currently, she is collaborating as the lead author on a horror franchise project with a top veteran Hollywood director and an award-winning screenwriter. When she's not immersed in books as an author, editor, and publishing professional, Ryan is an avid historical researcher, with specific interest in nautical and maritime history, cryptozoology, and ancient civilizations. She is represented by Gandolfo Helin & Fountain Literary Management. She also writes clean, seasonal romance under the name Lindy Miller. Ryan is a member of the Horror Writers Association, serves on the IBPA Board of Directors, and was a 2020 Publishers Weekly Star Watch Honoree.

Sumiko Saulson (Pronouns: ze/hir/hirs) is a writer of dark speculative fiction, and poetry, a cartoonist and zinemaker. Ze is an award-winning author of Afrosurrealist and multicultural sci-fi and horror, editor of the anthologies and collections *Black Magic Women*, *Scry of Lust*, *Black Celebration*, and *Wickedly Abled*, winner of the 2016 HWA StokerCon "Scholarship from Hell", 2017 BCC Voice "Reframing the Other" contest, 2017 Mixy Award, 2018 AWW "Afrosurrealist Writer Award," and 2020 HWA Diversity Grant recipient. Sumiko has an AA in English from Berkeley City College, and writes a column called "Writing While Black" for a national Black Newspaper, the San Francisco BayView. Ze is the host of the SOMA Leather and LGBT Cultural District's "Erotic Storytelling Hour." Ze can be found at www.SumikoSaulson.com, on Facebook, Twitter, and Tik-Tok @sumikoska and on Instagram @sumikosaulson.

E. F. Schraeder is the author of *Liar: Memoir of a Haunting* (Omnium

Gatherum, 2021) and the short story collection *Ghastly Tales of Gaiety and Greed* (Omnium Gatherum, 2020). A semi-finalist in Headmistress Press' 2019 Charlotte Mew Chapbook Contest, Schraeder work has appeared in a number of journals and anthologies.

Ingrid L. Taylor is a poet, science writer, and veterinarian whose poetry has recently appeared in the *Southwest Review*, the *Ocotillo Review*, *FERAL: A Journal of Poetry and Art*, *Horse Egg Literary*, and others. Her poem "Mermaids" received *Punt Volat Journal's* Annual Poetry Award in 2021. Her nonfiction work has appeared in Sentient Media. She's received support for her writing from the Playa Artist Residency, the Horror Writers Association, and Gemini Ink, and she received her MFA from Pacific University. Find her online at ingridltaylor.com.

Kailey Tedesco is the author of *She Used to be on a Milk Carton*, *Lizzie, Speak*, and *Foreverhaus* (April Gloaming Publishing & White Stag Publishing). She is a senior editor for *Luna Luna Magazine*, and she teaches an ongoing course on the archetype of the witch in literature at Moravian University. You can find her work featured in *Blood Bath Zine*, *Witch Craft Mag*, *Fairy Tale Review*, *Grimoire*, *Black Telephone Mag*, and more. For further information, please visit kaileytedesco.com.

Brenda S. Tolian is a member of HWA, HAG, and Denver Horror Collective. She earned her B.A. in English at Adams State University and her MFA from Regis University in Creative Writing, currently earning her Doctorate in Literature at Murray State University. Brenda is a lead instructor at Alchemy Writing Workshop in Dark Fiction. Her work appears in Haunted Mtl.com, the Anthology *101 Proof Horror,* the Denver Horror Collective's anthology *Consumed Tales Inspired by The Wendigo,* and *Twisted Pulp Magazine issue 3*. Her story "Ba' Lat Ov" will be coming out in *The Jewish Book of Horror,* and Raw Dog Screaming Press will publish her forthcoming book. She also co-hosts *Burial Plot*

Horror Podcast with Joy Yehle. She lives in and writes about the haunted high San Luis Valley surrounded by the Sangre de Cristo and the San Juan Mountain ranges—known for its cannibals, Skinwalkers, UFOs, cults, and vortexes.

Jacqueline West's work has appeared in *Mythic Delirium, Strange Horizons, Liminality, Mirror Dance,* and *Star*Line,* among other publications. Her first full-length collection of dark poetry, *Candle and Pins: Poems on Superstitions* was released in 2018. She is also the author of the New York Times-bestselling middle grade series *The Books of Elsewhere* and several other novels for young readers. Her 2019 YA horror novel, *Last Things,* was a finalist for the Minnesota Book Awards and a Ginger Nuts of Horror top twenty pick. Jacqueline lives with her family in Red Wing, Minnesota. www.jacquelinewest.com.

Sheldon Woodbury is an award-winning writer (screenplays, plays, books, short stories, and poems). His book *Cool Million* is considered the essential guide to writing high concept movies. His short stories and poems have appeared in many horror anthologies and magazines. His novel *The World on Fire* was published September, 2014 by JWK Fiction. His poem, "The Midnight Circus," was selected by Ellen Datlow as an honorable mention for Best Horror 2017.

Trisha J. Wooldridge writes stuff that occasionally wins awards—child-friendly ones as T.J. Wooldridge. Find her in the Shirley Jackson Award-winning *The Twisted Book of Shadows,* some *HWA Poetry Showcase* anthologies, all of the New England Horror Writer anthologies (that she didn't edit), *Don't Turn Out the Lights: A Tribute to Alvin Schwartz's Scary Stories to Tell in the Dark, Paranormal Contact: A Quiet Horror Confessional,* and the April 2021 issue of *34 Orchard* literary journal. She also lovingly tortures consenting authors with her editing talents, sometimes resulting in wickedly fantastic anthologies. She spends rare moments of mystical "free time" with a very patient Husband-of-

Awesome; a fluffy-tuxedoed, geriatric cat; a tiny witch kitty; and a matronly calico horse.www.anovelfriend.com.

Mercedes M. Yardley is a whimsical dark fantasist who wears poisonous flowers in her hair. She won the Bram Stoker Award for her story *Little Dead Red* and was a Bram Stoker Award nominee for her short story "Loving You Darkly" and the *Arterial Bloom* anthology. You can find her at mercedesmyardley.com.

Made in the USA
Columbia, SC
02 December 2021

50190138R00071